little Miss Fickle ™

by Roger Hargreaves

Copyright © 1984 by Roger Hargreaves
Published in U.S.A. by Price Stern Sloan, Inc.
11150 Olympic Boulevard, Suite 650, Los Angeles, California 90064
Printed in U.S.A. All rights reserved.
ISBN: 0-8431-1481-9

10 9 8

PRICE STERN SLOAN
Los Angeles

Would you like me to tell you a story?

If you were little Miss Fickle, you'd say "Yes"!

And then you'd say "No"!

And then, you'd say "Yes" again.

She was one of those people who just co[u]ld not make up their minds.

Ever!

About anything!

Little Miss Fickle lived in Dandelion Cottage on the outskirts of Sunnytown.

And she lived right next door to her best friend, little Miss Neat, who lived in Twopin Cottage.

One Monday little Miss Neat and little Miss Fickle went out to lunch in Sunnytown.

"I'll have the soup to start with," said little Miss Neat to the waiter as she looked at the menu, "followed by the fish."

"So will I," said little Miss Fickle.

But, after the waiter had written down the order, little Miss Fickle looked at the menu again.

"No, I won't," she said. "I'll have the salad followed by the meat!"

The waiter crossed out the first order, and wrote down the second.

"On the other hand," continued little Miss Fickle, "I won't have anything to start, and then I'll have the eggs."

The waiter sighed.

An hour later, when the waiter had worn out three pencils and four order pads, Miss Fickle finally finally decided to have the soup, followed by the fish.

The waiter brought the soup.

Little Miss Fickle looked at it.

"I'm not hungry," she said.

It was at that moment that the waiter decided he was going to be a bus conduc instead of a waiter.

On Tuesday, little Miss Fickle went to buy a hat.

"I want a new pink hat," she announced.

The salesgirl brought her two pink hats to choose from.

"I'll have this one," said Miss Fickle, after she had tried them both on.

"Certainly Madam," replied the salesgirl, and put it in a hatbox.

"On the other hand," said little Miss Fickle, "I think I'll have the other one!"

The salesgirl took the first hat out of the hatbox and put the second hat into the hatbox.

"But," continued Miss Fickle, "I think the first hat suited me better, don't you?"

The salesgirl didn't say anything as she took the second hat out of the hatbox and put the first hat into the hatbox.

She handed the hatbox to little Miss Fickle.

Miss Fickle looked at her.

"Do you have any blue hats?" she asked.

It was at that moment that the salesgirl decided she was going to be a secretary instead of a salesgirl!

On Wednesday, little Miss Fickle went to the butcher's.

"I'd like some sausages," she said.

"Beef or pork?" asked the butcher.

"Pork," replied Miss Fickle.

The butcher wrapped up the pork sausages

"But beef would be nice," said little Miss Fickle.

The butcher unwrapped the pork sausages, and wrapped up some beef sausages.

"On the other hand," continued Miss Fickle "chops would be better!"

It was at that moment that the butcher decided he needed a holiday.

But, on Thursday, guess what happened?

Little Miss Fickle disappeared!

Little Miss Neat had seen her pass Twopin Cottage on the way into Sunnytown, but she didn't come back.

She didn't come back on Friday either.

So Miss Neat went looking for her.

She met Mr. Muddle.

"Have you seen little Miss Fickle?" she asked, anxiously.

Mr. Muddle looked at her.

"Have I been for a little tickle?" he inquired.

"Oh, Mr. Muddle," she said, and hurried on.

She met Mr. Forgetful.

"Have you seen little Miss Fickle?" she asked him.

Mr. Forgetful thought.

"Well," she said. "Have you?"

"Have I what?" he asked.

"Oh, Mr. Forgetful," she said, and hurried on.

But, could she find little Miss Fickle?

She could not!

Nobody had seen her.

The Sunnytown Public Lending Library has nineteen thousand nine hundred and ninety-nine books.

On Saturday afternoon little Miss Fickle reached up and took one of them down from a shelf.

"I'll take this one," she thought to herself.

"On the other hand," she thought to herse looking at the book next to it on the shelf, "perhaps I'll take this one!"

She placed the first book back on to the shelf, and took down the other one.

It was the nineteen thousand nine hundred and ninety-ninth book she had chosen!

She'd been in the library for three days choosing a book!

Three whole days choosing one book!

She went home carrying it.

That Saturday afternoon, little Miss Neat was in the garden of Twopin Cottage wher little Miss Fickle walked past.

"Where have you BEEN?" she cried.

"At the library," replied little Miss Fickle.

"For THREE days?" exclaimed Miss Neat.

"Well," explained little Miss Fickle, "I wanted to choose the right book!"

And she held it up.

And then she stopped, and looked at it.

"Oh phooey," she said.
"I've read it!"